SOCCER STARS

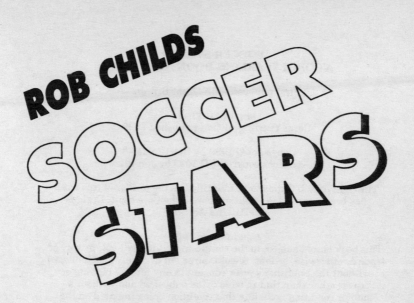

ROB CHILDS
SOCCER STARS

ILLUSTRATED BY
JON RILEY

CORGI YEARLING BOOKS

SOCCER STARS
A CORGI YEARLING BOOK : 0 440 863619

First publication in Great Britain

PRINTING HISTORY
Corgi Yearling edition published 1999

Set in 12/15pt Century Schoolbook
by Phoenix Typesetting, Ilkley, West Yorkshire.

Corgi Yearling Books are published by Transworld Publishers Ltd,
61–63 Uxbridge Road, Ealing, London W5 5SA,
in Australia by Transworld Publishers (Australia) Pty Ltd,
15–25 Helles Avenue, Moorebank, NSW 2170,
and in New Zealand by Transworld Publishers (NZ) Ltd,
3 William Pickering Drive, Albany, Auckland.

Made and printed in Great Britain by
Cox & Wyman Ltd, Reading, Berkshire.

For all budding young soccer stars

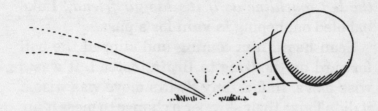

1 Sick as a Parrot

'The Swifts are on the attack again, inspired by the half-time pep talk from their player-manager, Luke Crawford. This is the last league game before Easter and we must . . . er, I mean, they must get a result today . . .'

It wasn't easy for the commentator to remain neutral. He was so involved in the match that he was actually playing in it as well.

Doing a running commentary was just one of Luke's many self-appointed roles for Swillsby Swifts. Besides being player-manager, he captained and coached the Under-13 Sunday

League side too. It was *his* team. He had formed it and signed up all the players. About the only thing he steered well clear of was washing their gold strip. He left that job to his mum.

'*The elegant Sean has the ball now, hugging the left touchline as if it's his girlfriend,*' Luke babbled on, hoping in vain for a pass.

Sean heard him coming and slipped the ball forward up the wing to Brain instead. It was a wise move. In fact, any Swifts move was wise if it didn't give their skipper a chance to mess it up. It was an unwritten club rule that would never be posted up on the changing cabin wall alongside many others: DON'T PASS TO LUKE.

'*The tricky winger takes on two defenders and weaves past both of them – super skills!*' continued the breathless commentary, undeterred. '*Brain cuts inside into the penalty area . . . it looks like he's going to shoot . . .*'

Brain had already shot while the words were still tumbling out of Luke's mouth. The Swifts' leading scorer was deadly with either foot and he unleashed a terrific strike with his right. The keeper only dived on top of the ball as it was bouncing back from the net.

'*GOOOAAALLL!!! The equalizer! Brain's done it again!*'

Luke's shriek of delight was a cue for the team celebrations to start. Players arrived from all over the pitch to mob the scorer and make fools of themselves in a wild war dance. Goals were something of a rare luxury for the Swifts and the boys liked to make the most of them.

'Great goal!' whooped Gary, their left wing-back, when they had finally calmed down a little. 'How many's that you've got now?'

Brain gave a shrug. 'Dunno. You'd better ask Luke.'

The skipper was bound to know. The details of every match were crammed into his notebook of soccer statistics. He kept a record of all the school games too in another book, even though his own appearances for Swillsby Comprehensive were few and far between. Luke didn't pick the Comp team.

'We've got 'em on the run,' he called out, shaking his fists to urge his teammates to greater efforts. 'C'mon, men, we can win this game now.'

'What's he going on about up there?' drawled Sanjay from his goal. 'Can't hear him.'

'You're not missing anything,' said Tubs, the Swifts' roly-poly full-back. 'Just the skipper's usual drivel.'

'Yeah, I know that. It's just that I'm collecting examples of his best drivel. I'm thinking of doing a piece on them for the school magazine. Should be a good laugh.'

'Concentrate!' Luke shouted. 'It's criminal to give away a soft goal straight after you've scored. You can get locked up for less than that.'

'There's another for my article,' Sanjay smirked. 'He's the one who ought to be locked up – for trying to play football while the balance of his mind is disturbed.'

'We know he's mad,' Tubs guffawed. 'Soccer mad!'

'Yeah, trouble is, I reckon we might all be getting as crazy as he is.'

The match was now level at 1–1, but the mood had swung in favour of the Swifts – and so had the blustery March wind. Its increasing strength helped to pin the visitors, Leeford Lions, in their own half.

'The Lions have lost their roar and are playing like lambs,' warbled the broadcaster in the number nine shirt. *'Every dog has his day, as they say, and the Swifts have got their tails up, sniffing the scent of the fox. These big cats are fast running out of lives . . .'*

Luke was in danger of running out of animals too as his cliché-ridden commentary became ever more bizarre. He'd already worked in allusions to giraffe-necks, tortoise shells, slippery eels and charging rhinoceros. As Tubs sent a hefty clearance upfield, Luke treated anyone within reception range to another four-legged simile. This time he likened their pacy right-winger to *'a greyhound springing out of its trap after the hare'.*

It was only because Dazza was the 100 metre sprint champion in his year group that he managed to catch the windswept ball and keep it in play near the corner flag. The slow full-back

had long given up such an unequal contest and Dazza found himself with only the Lions goalie for company.

Dazza did what he always did when he had the ball at his feet and time to think what to do with it. He panicked. Instead of dribbling nearer, he lashed the ball vaguely goalwards, slicing across it with the outside of his boot. The ball swerved and swirled in the wind, curling out of the keeper's reach into the top far corner of the net.

'One in a million!' cried Luke. 'A real stunner, Dazza. Bet you couldn't do that again if you tried.'

The skipper was probably right for once. Dazza could have spent the next few years practising the other 999,999 times without repeating his success.

As commentator, however, Luke was temporarily lost for words. He couldn't conjure up any creature that would quite serve to describe the wobbly flight path of such a fluke shot. He was just happy to join in the impromptu party hosted by the lucky lottery winner.

It was all too much. His previous warning about gift goals went unheeded. Mentally, the Swifts were still counting the unexpected riches of three points when the Lions carved through their non-existent defence to score an instant equalizer. Sanjay ruefully picked the ball out of the net, the first Swifts' player to touch it since Dazza's boomerang.

'I don't believe it!' sighed Luke. 'That was just so sloppy.'

'Never mind, skipper,' said Brain. 'We can always hope for another miracle.'

'Yeah, the Swifts winning would be a miracle,' said Gregg, Gary's identical twin. 'I can't remember what it feels like.'

To their credit, the Swifts did try their best to recover from the setback. But, as usual, their

best wasn't good enough. The goal had put the Lions back on top and, despite the gale, they gave Sanjay – and Tubs – several uncomfortable moments before the final whistle.

The Swifts survived by the width of a goalpost, the length of Sanjay's outstretched leg and then the ample dimensions of Tubs's midriff bulge. Leaning against the creaking post at a corner, Tubs took a shot full in the stomach and he doubled up on the line.

'Lost ball!' cried Gary. 'It's disappeared in Tubs's flab.'

As the referee blew for full-time, perhaps not wishing to go and search for the ball, the Swifts gathered around their winded, last-second saviour.

'Worth it, Tubs,' said Luke, failing to show too much sympathy. 'Saved a certain goal, that did, and let us hang on for a vital point.'

The defender's podgy face began to turn a delicate shade of green as Luke rambled on regardless. 'Shows how much we've improved this season, men. The Lions beat us 5–0 at their place before Christmas. Now we've got a draw against them. Bet they're feeling as sick as parrots right now . . .'

Tubs rolled over and noisily deposited the half-digested remains of his large lunch into Sanjay's upturned goalie cap that he kept behind the post.

'They're not the only ones,' murmured the goalkeeper in dismay.

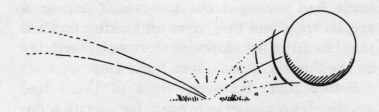

2   Home and Away

'Not wearing your cap, Sanjay?'

'Can I borrow it a minute? We've got a maths test after break.'

Sanjay had half-expected such attempts at coarse humour from his mates when he arrived at school next day. He ignored them and glanced at Tubs. 'Noticed you didn't offer to take the cap home and clean it up yourself.'

'Yeah, I'm fine now, thanks for asking,' Tubs replied sarcastically. 'Not my fault your stupid cap was lying there. I didn't do it on purpose.'

'Wouldn't put it past you.'

Aside from the contents of Sanjay's cap, there were two other main topics of conversation during the last week of term. The most important one for the Swifts was the exciting prospect of going away on a weekend tour. Luke's dad and uncle had arranged the two-match trip as a special treat and they were all looking forward to celebrating the skipper's thirteenth birthday on the Sunday. It was April Fools Day!

Before that, however, some of them had another big occasion to prepare for – a cup semifinal for the school on Thursday afternoon. Swillsby Comprehensive's grumpy sports teacher, 'Frosty' Winter, had relied heavily on one simple tactic in steering his limited Year 8 squad through the early rounds of the competition. It basically boiled down to not having too many Swifts in the team, and especially not Luke Crawford.

His small pool of players meant that certain choices were often forced upon him. Sanjay, for instance, was the only recognized goalkeeper in the year group, even though the likeness was somewhat tenuous. And speaking of likenesses, the reason both the Garner twins were regulars for the Comp was that Frosty still couldn't tell them apart.

He only had himself to blame for the shortage of available talent. His notorious short fuse and lashing tongue had driven several of the better footballers away. Much to the teacher's chagrin, Luke appeared to be immune to the effects of *Frostbite*, as they called it.

The boy's passion for the game meant that all Frosty's best efforts to humiliate and ridicule him had failed to work. Even attempted murder in the changing room would be unlikely to make Luke miss a practice session. It might only delay his arrival for a few minutes while he wriggled free of the rope that suspended him from the shower fittings.

Luke was the first one in the training grids as usual at the start of Tuesday's practice. He dribbled a ball around inside one of the square grids by himself, feigning to sell dummies to invisible opponents. More often than not, his quick turns left him on his backside when his feet became clumsily entangled.

'*And here we see Luke Crawford sharpening up his skills for the Swifts' Easter tour . . .*' burbled the commentary softly. Luke had spotted some of the others approaching and lowered the volume, '*. . . he shields the ball cleverly with his body, then throws his opponent off-balance with*

a sudden twist and darts away . . . oops!'

'What yer doing, sitting in the mud, Luke?' Gary called out.

'Just having a rest, waiting for you lot,' he replied casually. 'What's kept you?'

'Frosty's been sorting out transport and stuff with us for Thursday.'

'I didn't know he was going to be doing that.'

The players glanced at each other and smirked. 'No, I think he waited till you'd dashed out the changing room,' Gregg confessed. 'You know what he's like.'

Luke sighed and scrambled to his feet. 'Has the team been announced?' he asked, trying to keep any note of hope out of his voice. He was almost resigned to missing out on the semi-final. He hadn't played for the Comp for weeks, not even as a substitute.

His cousin Jon, the Comp's star striker and captain, answered. 'Soz, Luke, 'fraid there's no place for you. I did put in a good word, but . . .'

'Yeah, I know, Johan, thanks. C'mon, you can have some shooting practice at me in goal before Frosty gets here and spoils things.'

Luke loved watching his cousin in action. Jon's enviable ball skills seemed to come so naturally to him, just as they once did to Johan Cruyff, the most gifted player in the star-studded Dutch team of the 1970s. It was little wonder that Luke had nicknamed Jon after his all-time soccer hero.

If Jon was poetry in motion on the football field, Luke in comparison was more like a tedious comprehension exercise. But he was still hugging himself at his own recent stroke of genius. He had persuaded Jon to desert his crack Sunday League side this weekend and 'guest' for the Swifts on tour. The Padley Panthers had reluctantly given their consent, provided that

Jon only played on one of the days.

'You looking forward to the tour, Johan?' asked Luke after he retrieved one of his shots from the tangled netting.

'Sure,' came back the reply. 'Should be great fun.'

'Yeah, but it's serious, too, you know. I'd like to win both matches. Winning's a good habit for a team. It'll help us in our crucial league games after Easter. You want to play Saturday or Sunday?'

'Up to you, Luke . . . or is that Skipper?' grinned Jon, referring to his cousin's preferred term of address on Swifts' duty. 'I'll play in whichever game you think I'm most needed. You're the boss.'

That was sweet music to Luke's ears. He just wished the others might be so respectful. Frosty certainly wasn't when he appeared on the scene.

'Right, you lot, let's get cracking. No time to mess around in these grids. I want to practise some corners. Brain, you take them from both sides. Luke, you act as ball boy behind the goal...'

Luke didn't bother travelling to watch the semifinal. He would get all the details from Jon later. He had better things to do with his time – like deciding on tactics and formations for the Swifts' two tour matches.

As soon as he arrived home from school, he went up to his bedroom and switched on the computer. He needed to finish off compiling the tour dossier and print out a copy for each member of the squad. It would normally have been a totally absorbing labour of love, but he found it strangely difficult to concentrate. His mind kept straying on to the Comp's cup-tie.

'Wonder what's happening?' he murmured, checking the time again. 'Should be well into the second half by now. Hope we make the Final. Quite fancy playing in that and winning a medal...'

At that very moment, the Comp were desperately clinging on to a 1–0 lead, given to them by Gregg on the stroke of half-time. He'd scrambled the ball over the line after the goalkeeper had parried a shot from Brain, the one Swifts' player that Frosty was glad to have in his side.

'C'mon, ref, blow that whistle,' the teacher urged, jabbing at his watch. 'Time's up.'

It was wishful thinking. There were still several minutes to go and Frosty doubted whether the Comp could hold out for much longer. Their goal had been under almost constant pressure throughout the second period, but somehow remained intact. Sanjay was having one of his better – or luckier – days.

'Here they come again,' the goalkeeper cried as the home team launched yet another attack in search of the equalizer. 'Mark up tight, defence.'

The winger slipped the ball through Gary's legs and thumped over a high centre to the far post where the number ten was lurking, completely unmarked. Sanjay might as well have saved his breath, but at least he did manage to save the header. He leapt across his goal in spectacular fashion and plucked the ball out of the air with both hands.

'Boot it right away upfield,' yelled Frosty. 'Anywhere will do. Just get rid of the thing.'

Sanjay was annoyed at the lack of praise and threw the ball out instead to Big Ben, the gangly Swifts' centre-back who had come on as a substitute. Big Ben wasn't expecting it and Sanjay's warning shout came too late to prevent the loose ball from being collected by an attacker.

With Sanjay out of position, the goal was at his mercy. The boy was so certain he was going to score that he delayed his shot, savouring the moment. All he had to do was roll . . .

No-one quite knew where Gary came from, or how he got there in time. One second Frosty was cursing, the next he was astonished to see the

ball whipped off the striker's toes by Gary's last-ditch sliding tackle.

The groans of disappointment from the home supporters soon turned to howls of dismay. Brain had broken away up the left wing and pierced the defence with a through pass to Jon who supplied the *coup de grâce*. The ball was struck first time, on the run, and snaked low into the bottom corner of the net.

Instead of facing a replay, the Comp were now 2–0 up and the match was as good as over. They had booked their place in the Final.

It was a rare smile indeed that began to creep across the unfamiliar territory of Frosty's stubbled face. Not knowing which way to go, it soon lost its nerve and quickly disappeared. Jon thought he might just have seen it, but put it down to a trick of the light.

That really would have been something to tell Luke to record in his little black book. *The day that Frosty smiled*. Jon reckoned his cousin might have had more difficulty in believing that than the actual scoreline.

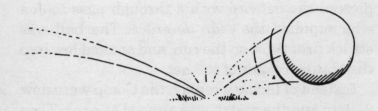

3   On Tour

'Typical!' grumbled Sanjay. 'Didn't take long for things to go wrong.'

'Yeah, at least it normally waits till after we kick off,' said Sean.

The goalkeeper sighed. 'We'll be lucky if the whole tour isn't jinxed, with you-know-who helping to organize it.'

'Might even have to be called off at this rate.'

'Oh, don't say that!' cried Brain. 'We've all been looking forward to this trip for weeks. Y'know, going off on tour like real footballers do.'

'Well, guess this is just about as close as most

of us will ever get to being *real* footballers,' grunted Tubs, looking around them. 'Sitting on a pavement kerb in Padley, five miles from home.'

The Swifts had stopped to pick up Luke's Italian cousin, Ricki, and their hired minibus clearly didn't fancy the rest of the journey. As they tried to set off again, the engine had stuttered, whined and died.

'I thought this old crate had complained a bit when Tubs climbed on board,' remarked Gary.

'Can't say I blame it,' put in his twin. 'And then adding another Crawford was just too much for it.'

'I am not a Crawford,' Ricki protested. 'My name is Fortuna.'

'Yeah, yeah, we know that, Ricki,' said Gregg. 'But you're half a Crawford. You can't help it if your mum comes from a disaster-prone family. They've got the *Sadim* touch.'

'Sadim?'

'That's Midas in reverse. Everything they touch turns to dross!'

'Like the Swifts,' muttered Big Ben. 'Having four and a half Crawfords on this tour was just asking for trouble.'

'Hey, I heard that,' Jon butted in, grinning.

'Soz, Jon, you must be the exception. You *have* got the golden touch!'

Luke and his dad had gone off with Jon's dad to the hire company in town to seek a replacement vehicle. Uncle Ray's large estate car was also being used to ease the overcrowding on the bus, with luggage stuffed into the back and strapped on to the roofrack.

'They went plenty time ago,' said Ricki. 'We will be late for kick-off s'afto.'

'Your English is getting better than mine,' said Tubs. 'When are you off back to sunny Italy?'

'Soon, I think. We only came for few months, y'know.'

'You'll still be here after Easter, won't you?'

'I hope so. Plenty important games to play, yes?'

'Dead right, there, Ricki,' said Big Ben. 'Luke won't let you out of the country till the end of the season. He still believes we can avoid finishing bottom of the league.'

'Perhaps we wouldn't be in the mess we are if you'd been able to play for us more often,' said Sanjay. 'Not seen you for ages.'

Ricki shrugged and spread his hands. 'My father, he wants me to play rugby on Sundays.

Is difficult, y'know, but rugby is over now. I am free as . . . how you say . . . a budgie.'

'Yeah, close. Something like that,' the goal-keeper replied and then jumped to his feet. 'Hey! Look, they've got a new bus.'

Judging by its appearance, not to mention the registration plate, the 'new' minibus was even older than the original.

'Huh! No expense spared, I see, Skipper,' said Tubs as Luke clambered out of the creaking back door. 'Not exactly the latest model, is it?'

Luke pulled a face. 'This was all they'd got left on a Saturday morning so don't knock it.'

'I wouldn't dare. Things might drop off.'

'We haven't got time to hang around while they fix the first one. It was either this or nothing.'

Tubs eyed the bus suspiciously. 'I think you made the wrong choice.'

There was a stampede for any spare places in Ray's car before the boys reluctantly began to reload their belongings into the bus. They were reassured to find that at least it was fitted with seat belts.

'Sorry about the delay,' said Philip, Luke's dad, clasping himself into the driver's seat. 'Next stop, Tibworth, for our first match.'

'Next stop, lunch, I hope,' said Tubs. 'I'm starving.'

Ray's packed estate car led the minibus along the tree-lined drive through the grounds of Tibworth Manor.

'Cool!' breathed Jon. 'Is this where Tibworth All Stars play?'

The country mansion at last came into view and his dad grinned. 'Bit grander than Swillsby recky, eh? The chap who runs the All Stars owns this place. He was a pro footballer himself once, apparently.'

'Sounds like we might need you today, Jon,' said Sean.

''Fraid not. Luke's decided to save me till tomorrow.'

'That's crazy!' protested Mark, Big Ben's partner in central defence.

'That's Luke for you!' agreed Sean, giggling.

As the vehicles scrunched to a halt in the gravelled car park, a man came out of the house. He strode towards them, limping slightly, his grim face showing no intention of offering hospitality to the travellers.

'My name's Miller – coach of the All Stars,' he called out brusquely as the two drivers emerged. 'Almost given you lot up.'

'Sorry we're late,' replied Philip Crawford. 'Had a breakdown.'

Sanjay couldn't resist making a loud comment from the rear of the bus. 'Yeah, a mental one, putting up with us all season.'

The coach did not seem to appreciate the joke. 'Tell yer players to get a move on. I'm a busy man. I just hope you're worth the wait.'

'Nice bloke,' muttered Ray as the coach turned away.

Luke had been studying him carefully. 'Sure I've seen that guy somewhere before. What did he say his name was?'

'Miller, I think,' said Gary. 'C'mon, let's go and get changed. I'm in a hurry too. I'm desperate for the toilet.'

As everyone piled out of the minibus, Luke was still preoccupied over the puzzle. Then, in the distance, he saw the coach kick some practice balls onto the pitch and the penny suddenly dropped. And so did his jaw.

'Of course – Robbie Miller!'

'Who's Robbie Miller when he's at home?' asked Tubs.

Mark overheard him. 'He *is* at home. This is his front garden!'

'You must have heard of Robbie Miller!' Luke exclaimed.

The Swifts looked at him blankly. Even his dad and uncle admitted that the name didn't mean much to them. Luke could scarcely believe it.

'Robbie Miller was only one of Scotland's greatest players back in the Sixties,' he stated. 'Along with people like Denis Law and Jim Baxter.'

'Oh, I've heard of them all right,' said Dad. 'Brilliant, they were.'

'So was Robbie Miller. Well, till he broke his leg, anyway, playing in the F.A. Cup Final one year. I've got loads of pictures of him in my old soccer annuals. Must get his autograph.'

Sanjay laughed. 'You're a mine of useless information, Skipper. I've no idea how you remember every little detail like you do. Bet you know more about his career than he does.'

'Don't encourage him,' groaned Tubs. 'We'll be here all day.'

Gary couldn't bear the thought of that. He was off, wriggling his way towards the changing rooms. When the rest of the squad reached there, they discovered that their skipper's memory was

not infallible. He had forgotten his football boots.

Luke was mortified. 'Must've left them in that other bus,' he wailed. 'What am I gonna do? I can't play in trainers.'

'You can borrow mine,' Jon offered. 'We take the same size.'

'Really? Your boots!' cried Luke in amazement. 'Don't you mind?'

Jon laughed. 'Why should I? There's nothing special about them.'

'It's what's inside the boots that counts,' said

Uncle Ray proudly. 'Perhaps Jon's goal-scoring magic will rub off on you today, Luke, eh?'

The first thing Luke did in Jon's boots was to win the toss. 'A lucky omen,' he murmured and then switched into commentary mode.

'The Swifts' skipper, Luke Crawford, has decided to kick towards the manor in the first half, hoping to use the wind. He wants his team to make a good impression in this opening match of their tour. Especially now in front of the great Robbie Miller. A good start is so important . . .'

The All Stars obviously agreed. After five minutes, Luke's borrowed boots had only had one kick each, and that was to restart the game. Sanjay had touched the ball just twice too, performing his regular job of fishing the ball out of the back of his net.

The Swifts' hapless goalkeeper was good at doing that. He'd had lots of practice all season.

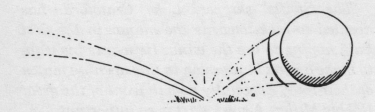

4   Star-struck

By half-time, the Swifts were 7–0 down.

Luke was about to launch into his usual frantic team talk when Robbie Miller trudged past. 'You lot aren't fit to play on here,' he snarled. 'Some great footballers have graced this pitch over the years.'

There was no way of responding to that insult. They simply had to take it on the chin. Sean broke the embarrassed silence after Miller had gone.

'Charming! If that guy's rich enough to own all this, he ought to be able to afford some manners.'

'Our Mr Miller may not be as well off as it appears,' said Ray. 'I've just been speaking to one of their lads' parents. He reckons that Miller's business has gone bust recently. Might even have to sell up.'

Luke gazed around the expanse of land in front of the house, most of which was marked out with soccer pitches. To Luke, it seemed like Paradise. 'Fancy having to leave a place like this. That's terrible.'

'Don't start getting any ideas,' Dad chuckled, seeing the look in his eye. 'You'll be wanting me to buy it off him and move in!'

'I trust you're not still gonna ask Miller for his autograph,' said Titch, Swifts' miniature midfielder.

'Might do,' Luke said with a shrug. 'Anyway, it's up to us to make him eat his words. If we snatch an early goal in the second half, you never know what might happen. Football's a funny old game, as they say.'

'Whoever says that has never played in goal for the Swifts,' muttered Sanjay. 'They'd have lost their sense of humour ages ago.'

'We've got to keep our heads up, men,' Luke told them, ignoring Sanjay's remark. 'Show them we're not gonna go down without a fight.'

'Ever the optimist, our skipper,' said Gregg. 'He'd make the end of the world seem like a good chance to make a fresh start.'

'Well, the end of the world's not the end of the world, is it?'

'Eh?'

'I mean, there's always tomorrow.'

'Tomorrow never comes,' grunted Titch.

'I hope it does this weekend – it's my birthday! And we've got another match tomorrow as well, remember. Jon's playing in that one.'

'Pity he's not playing now,' said Sean. 'Why can't we just bring him on?'

''Cos the skipper's whipped his boots for one thing,' cackled Sanjay.

'Fat lot of good they are without Jon in them. They're just running about all over the place, getting in everybody's way.'

Luke gave Sean a dirty look. 'You know we're only allowed to play Jon on one of the days. That was part of the loan deal with Panthers.'

'Who's gonna tell them? Jon and his dad won't let on.'

'That's not the point. The thing is . . .'

The argument was ended by the referee's whistle and the group broke up before Luke could explain. He was used to that. His team

talks were always being interrupted. He hadn't managed to finish one all season.

There *was* an early goal soon after the restart, but unfortunately not for the Swifts. Sanjay made a complete hash of catching a cross and the number nine tapped the ball over the line for his hat-trick. And then he scored again – and again. Once they had reached double figures, the All Stars turned their team upside down. All the substitutes came on and the keeper swapped places with the five-goal centre-forward. Despite these changes, the score kept mounting, and even the ex-keeper netted twice.

The Swifts left their comeback rather too late. In the dying minutes of the game, Brain at last opened their account with a delicate chip over the sub goalie's head, and then Ricki headed home a corner to make it 13–2. Only the scorer got excited about the goal. Ricki was so carried away, he gathered the ball up and placed it for a conversion attempt.

But there was someone else who would never give up, not until the final whistle, and maybe not even then – the indefatigable skipper. Luke collected a stray ball inside his own penalty area and decided to go on a run. The amused All Stars stood by and let it happen.

'The skipper's on the ball now, gliding over the halfway line as space appears in front of him. The opposition has backed off, giving him the respect he deserves. Their defence has opened up like the Red Sea . . .'

Even Luke, at the back of his fertile mind, might have begun to suspect that something wasn't quite right. He'd never been allowed so much time on the ball in his whole career. Somebody normally took it off him within a few seconds, and often it was one of his own teammates.

Time and space seemed to lose reality, as if in a dream. It felt like he was the only player on the pitch. His vision narrowed to the blinkered tunnel ahead of him – and the light at the end of it was the goal itself.

He only tripped over the ball once as he dribbled along, unchallenged, but he still had time to pick himself up and carry on. Suddenly, almost unexpectedly, he found himself in the All Stars goalmouth. He just had the keeper to beat – and even he was leaning on the post. Luke was confused.

'Shoot first, ask questions later,' he decided and then shot.

The ball hit the other post, but luckily bounced

back towards him. He was able to control it, stumble, steady himself again and slice the rebound just wide of the smirking keeper into the net.

'GOOAALL!' he roared and turned, arms aloft, to celebrate.

'Sorry, no goal,' said the referee. 'I'd already blown the whistle.'

'What for? I can't have been offside. I've just run the length of the field.'

'I know. We've all been watching. I blew for the end of the game. They think it's all over – and they're right, it is.'

Luke turned a deep crimson. 'I didn't hear anything,' he said lamely.

The referee smiled. 'Not surprised, lad, the way you were talking to yourself. Still, it's no crime to be so wrapped up in the game.'

Luke trailed away behind his sniggering teammates towards the changing rooms. 'You could have done something to stop me,' he moaned to his dad.

'You were too far gone. Nobody could get a word in edgeways past your commentary. You pretending to be this Bobby Miller or somebody?'

'*Robbie* Miller,' Luke stressed. 'He hated anybody calling him Bobby. Always insisted on

Robbie. It's more Scottish, you see.'

'Well, here he comes now, this *Robbie*, and he still doesn't look too happy. This may not be the best time to ask for his autograph.'

The All Stars coach jabbed a finger at his mobile phone. 'Last time *they* get invited here, I'll see to that,' he was heard to mutter.

He glared at Luke and his dad for a moment before forcing a smile on to his craggy face.

'Look,' began Philip, 'I'm sorry if we . . .'

'Och! Doesna matter now,' said Miller. 'Your Sparrows at least played with a bit o' spirit, kept going right to the end – just like I used to do. Canna stand any team that gives up.'

'Um . . . we're called the *Swifts*, Mr Miller,' Luke said timidly, hoping the great man wouldn't mind being corrected, and then piled on the flattery. 'You were a terrific player, I've read all about you. The way you inspired that famous Scottish win at Wembley, and that brilliant goal you scored in the Cup Final before you got injured . . .'

Luke might have gone on further. He had a knowledge of the game's history as deep as an anorak's pockets, all zipped up so that no tiny detail could ever escape. Miller cut him short.

'Aye, but we still lost – and I never did get a

cup-winners' medal,' he said bitterly and then gave Luke a quizzical look. 'I'm amazed such a wee laddie knows things like that about me nowadays. What's my first name?'

'Robbie, of course,' Luke replied instantly and seized his chance. 'Um . . . please may I have your autograph?'

Miller grinned and pulled out a piece of paper and a pen from his coat pocket to scrawl his name. 'Aye, good job you got that right,' he said, handing over the paper. 'Now, as an extra reward, how would you like to see a lot more old soccer stars tomorrow?'

Luke's excited, flushed face made any words unnecessary and Miller explained his offer. 'I've

organized a wee seven-a-side tournament here in the morning – for charity, y'ken – and I've just had a call from one of the teams. They've cried off and let me down at the last minute. What about you and your Sparrows coming along to make up the numbers, eh?'

Luke overlooked the Sparrows reference this time. 'That'd be brilliant, Mr Miller. You mean, actually play against all the old stars?'

Miller laughed. 'I don't think you're quite up to that, laddie. No, the veterans are putting on an exhibition game to pull in the crowds and raise more money. Their autographs won't come free like mine.'

Philip Crawford tried to curb his son's enthusiasm. 'Well, I'm not sure we could get back tomorrow, Mr Miller. 'You see . . .'

'Plenty of time, Dad,' Luke said quickly. 'We haven't got far to go for the afternoon match, have we? And besides, it *is* my birthday!'

'Right, that's settled,' said Miller. 'Be here ten o'clock sharp for the first match.'

'Can we have our pictures taken with a famous player?' asked Luke, star-struck but not tongue-tied.

Miller's reply, however, left him totally gob-smacked. 'Far better than that, laddie. We've got

something very special coming here tomorrow too. Something even I've never got my hands on before.'

'What's that?' he said breathlessly, hardly daring to guess the answer.

'The F.A. Cup!'

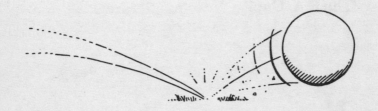

5   Bumps in the Night

Room 13 was as dark as a dungeon, but nobody in the six-bed dormitory was asleep. And it wasn't just the sound of Tubs crunching his way through a packet of chocolate biscuits that kept the boys awake.

'It's only a stupid story,' he spluttered, sitting up among the crumbs in his bottom bunk. 'I mean, everybody knows ghosts don't exist.'

'Yeah, right, but even so . . . what if there really was a double murder in this room . . . ?' came a less confident voice from above. Titch hadn't let the heavyweight defender claim the top bunk in case it collapsed and squashed him flat during the night. He'd then needed Tubs's help to clamber up into bed.

His question hung in the air like a bad smell. The possible answer to it was something that had been troubling the footballers ever since the hostel manager had told them the old building was supposed to be haunted.

'Do you reckon the guy was having us on?' asked Gary.

'Well, if he was, it ain't very funny,' muttered his brother below him. 'Why did he have to say it was twin boys that got killed in here?'

'Serves you right,' Brain hissed. 'It was you two who started all this nonsense in the first place, pretending you'd seen a ghost on the stairs. He probably heard you going on about it at tea-time.'

'Look, just shut up, all of you,' demanded Luke. 'Try to get some sleep. We've got a big day ahead of us tomorrow.'

'*Today*, you mean,' Gregg corrected him, peering at the luminous dial of his watch. 'It's just gone midnight.'

Luke's roommates broke into a raucous chorus of '*Happy Birthday, Dear Skipper!*' which helped to take their minds off ghosts, if nothing else.

 53

'Let's celebrate,' cried Tubs. 'I've got a sponge cake in my bag. We can't spend a night in a dorm without having a midnight feast, can we? It's a kind of tradition, like.'

'Just an excuse to feed your fat face again,' laughed Gary as Tubs swung his feet out of bed to fetch the cake.

'Fancy having your thirteenth birthday in room 13,' put in Brain. 'You could even wear the number 13 shirt in the match, Skipper.'

'No, thanks,' snorted Luke. 'I've had enough of Frosty giving me that number for the Comp this season.'

'You've said your precious Johan Cruyff always wore number 14 on his back, even before the days of squad numbers,' Gary reminded him.

'That's different. He was special. He wrote his own rules. He was allowed to wear what he liked.'

Their banter was suddenly interrupted by a loud drumming on the door and the room went very quiet. Tubs even stopped cutting up the cake he was about to share out. Luke waited for Dad's voice telling them to keep the noise down, but the warning failed to come.

'W . . . who is it?' he stuttered. 'W . . . what do you want?'

There was no response and Tubs lost his patience. 'Bet it's just some of the others messing about, trying to scare us.'

'They're doing a good job of it too,' Gary whispered. 'I'm not going near that door.'

'Well I am,' said Tubs, brandishing the cake knife. 'If I catch whoever it is, I'll kill 'em.'

'They might already be dead,' snuffled Brain. 'Careful, Tubs.'

'It's a very brave ghost who dares to get between Tubs's belly and his food,' said Gregg. 'That's asking for it.'

Tubs flapped across the cold dormitory floor in bare feet, but he never reached the door. The lights began to flash on and off and eerie music could be heard in the corridor. Tubs scuttled back to bed, scattering cake and biscuits everywhere. His panicky flight seemed strangely slowed in the stroboscopic lighting effect, making his rotund figure look like a gyrating hippo in a disco.

The music faded, the lights went out and the rapping ceased. The dormitory held its collective breath, as if expecting something to appear round or even through the door. But if it did, none of its occupants saw it. Nobody was looking, heads hidden under blankets or pillows.

Many minutes passed before Gary nervously risked a peep. 'Er . . . I think it's gone – whatever it was.'

'Go and take a look,' urged his twin.

'You must be joking . . .' he began and then realized that Gregg was next to him in the same bunk. 'Get back down to your own bed, you nutter. What yer doing up here?'

'Dunno, guess it just seemed safer higher up.'

Very little sleep was snatched that night. Even Tubs had lost his appetite, nibbling on a few salvaged biscuits merely for comfort. Only as the first rays of dawn filtered through the curtains did the room feel more normal and the boys manage to doze off.

Not Luke. He was lying on his bunk and gazing at a sheet of paper he had pulled from under his pillow where he'd put it for safe keeping. In the dim light, he could just make out Robbie Miller's autograph.

'Think I'll buy an autograph book with some of my birthday money,' he decided. 'I can make a great start to my collection with Miller and those other old soccer stars too. Maybe I'll even get Johan's one day . . .'

Dreamily, he turned the paper over and saw that there was a sketch map and some writing

on the back. 'Wonder what all this is about?' he mused, sliding his hand under the pillow again to fumble for his little torch. 'Might be important . . .'

It was. But it took Luke's sleep-starved mind several minutes of study in the torchlight to work out just how important. He could barely read the scribbled notes, making out a mention of the F.A. Cup and a million pounds. It was the word *pirates* that puzzled him.

As the shocking truth hit home, a chill ran down his spine. He sat bolt upright. All thoughts of his birthday and even the tour fled in panic. His hands were shaking.

'I don't believe it!' he gasped aloud. 'No, surely not . . .'

At that precise moment, the door burst open. Before Luke could react, he was hauled bodily off his bunk and bundled out of the room. The intruders were no terrifying phantoms. Just a pyjama-clad group of laughing players from another dormitory.

His torch had clattered to the floor, but Luke still clung on to the sheet of paper. He shrieked his protests, waking everyone else up, as they half-dragged, half-carried him along the corridor towards the washroom.

'Let's give him the birthday bumps first,' Sanjay cried over the noise of a gushing shower.

There was nothing Luke could do to stop them. Gripped by half-a-dozen teammates, he was subjected to a limb-wrenching, stomach-churning series of uncoordinated lifts and falls. The count seemed to go on for ever.

'. . . ten . . . eleven . . . twelve . . . and . . . thirteen!' they chanted, almost dropping him by the end through exhaustion.

If Luke thought the ordeal was over, he was wrong.

'Right, now dunk him in here quick,' gasped Big Ben, pulling wide the shower curtain.

The skipper was manhandled across the tiles and forced under the icy cold jets of water. At least he had the satisfaction of making sure that his kidnappers got soaking wet too as they struggled to keep him in place.

'Happy birthday, Skipper!' they cackled before finally letting him escape from his freezing water torture and tossing him a towel.

'Best way to start a day,' sniggered Sanjay, drying his own hair. 'A cold shower really wakes you up.'

'I already *was* awake,' Luke complained, shivering, pulling off the saturated top that clung to him like a second skin. 'Bet it was thanks to you lot I never even got any sleep at all.'

'No idea what you're talking about,' said Big Ben.

'Don't act so innocent. You know what I mean. Acting stupid with the light and music and everything at midnight.'

'Fast asleep we were then, Skip,' said Dazza. 'Never heard a thing.'

Luke suddenly lost interest in their denials. He bent down and picked up a soggy mess from the bottom of the shower cubicle.

'Oh, no!' he groaned. 'Look at this. You've ruined it.'

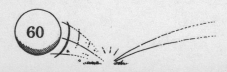

'Sorry, Skip. What was it? Anything special?'

Luke was devastated. The paper tore into shreds as he tried to open it up. He hadn't just lost Miller's autograph. He'd lost all proof of the Scottish star's outrageous plans to steal the F.A. Cup!

6   Birthday Boy

'April Fool!'

'Grow up, will yer!' protested Tubs, finding out too late that there was a layer of salt in the sugar bowl.

Gary laughed. 'You don't mind having a bit of salt on your cornflakes, do you?'

'Yes, I do. April Fool pranks are for little kids.'

'You mean like my kid brother,' he smirked, enjoying the superiority of an extra ten minutes' breathing time over his twin. Gregg had caught him out before breakfast by tying the legs of Gary's jeans into a knot.

The smirk suddenly disappeared. Over the hubbub of voices in the hostel's dining room, Gary had become aware of the sound of music. He grabbed Tubs's arm, making him spill his tea onto the table cloth.

'I'm warning you – cut it out . . .'

Then Tubs heard the music too and stood up, searching for the source.

'Sit down,' Titch complained. 'You're blocking out the light.'

'Shut up and listen. That's what we heard when the ghosts . . .'

Ray Crawford strutted into the room carrying a cassette player. 'Like my soothing music, boys?' he asked with a huge grin.

'Was that you?' demanded his nephew. 'All that banging and stuff?'

'April Fool!' he cried. 'Hope it didn't scare you too much.'

'No, course not,' Gary lied. 'We knew it was somebody playing a joke on us. Gave us a good laugh too, didn't it, Skipper?'

Luke's muttered agreement did not sound very convincing and his dad handed him a parcel. 'Happy birthday, Luke – your first day as a teenager. I trust this will make up for any lost beauty sleep last night.'

Luke tore open the wrapping paper and held up an orange football shirt for all to see. He had a Holland kit at home, but the style was out of date and the number nine shirt was now a bit small for him. This one was emblazoned with the name CRUYFF above his hero's legendary number 14. The room dissolved into laughter.

Luke's pleasure at the gift was diluted by the dark cloud that hung over him. He'd hardly tasted his breakfast, too busy brooding about the threat to the F.A. Cup. He still hadn't told anybody what he thought Miller was up to. The

incriminating evidence had been washed away.

'Thanks, Dad,' he managed to say. 'Just what I wanted. Pity I'm not fourteen today, I guess.'

'Superstar!' cried Sanjay. 'With that shirt and Jon's boots, there'll be no stopping our skipper now.'

'Yeah, but Jon needs his boots back today,' Sean pointed out.

'Hope so. What's the squad for the Sevens, Skipper?' the goalkeeper asked. 'Have you sorted it out yet?'

Luke sighed. He'd almost forgotten about the tournament. Deciding on which players and tactics to employ had helped him to while away the sleepless hours, but it now all seemed so trivial.

'Well, there's me of course,' he began, 'then cousins Jon and Ricki . . .'

'This is starting to sound like a family show,' Tubs guffawed. 'You'll be telling us next that your dad and uncle are turning out too!'

'Does that mean I can't play this afternoon now?' Jon piped up.

'No problem, the way I see it,' Luke explained. 'The Panthers only banned you from playing both days. They said nothing about you not playing twice on the same day.'

'Nice one, Boss,' Jon smiled.

'Anyway, I've picked an eight-man squad, so the rest are Sanjay, Brain, Big Ben, Gary and Titch. We'll use a basic 2–2–2 formation, OK?'

Nobody could be bothered to argue. They rarely kept to their positions during a game in any case. Even Sanjay had been known to wander upfield at times for a strike at the other goal.

As the boys left the dining room, Gary went up to Ray. 'Er ... there is just one thing I've been wondering about. How did you do the trick with the flashing lights?'

'Never touched the light switch,' he replied, puzzled. 'You must have been imagining that ...'

*

The Swifts arrived at Tibworth Manor to find the playing area already swarming with people. Some of those wearing soccer boots were also in fancy dress. They were college students out to have fun and raise money for charity at the same time. All the teams in the different age-group competitions were being sponsored for every goal scored.

There were teams of cowboys and indians, pantomime dames, spacemen, animals and teddy bears, and even a side made up of seven

Elvis Presleys. But the group of players that immediately caught Luke's eye was the one in pirate outfits.

'Glad you made it on time, Sparrows,' Robbie Miller welcomed them as they reported in. 'Your first match is on that far pitch.'

'Nobody told us we were supposed to be sponsored,' said Ray.

'I'll sponsor you myself. What shall we say – a hundred pounds a goal?' he chuckled and the boys gasped. 'From what I saw of you Sparrows yesterday, I don't reckon it's gonna cost me very much.'

A helicopter appeared out of the clouds and Miller squinted up towards it. 'Aye, good, right on cue. You can all do your bit by paying to pose with this.'

'What, the chopper?' said Sanjay.

'Nay, what's inside it, laddie. Had it flown in, special delivery.'

The helicopter circled the grounds twice and came down to settle on a landing pad next to the manor. Before the blades had even stopped whirling, a security guard stepped out with a gleaming trophy cradled in his burly arms.

'Wow! Just look at that,' cried Brain in excitement. 'The F.A. Cup!'

'What a treat for the birthday boy!' grinned Sanjay. 'We'll never hear the last of this.'

The Cup was placed on a display table near the pitches and a queue immediately began to form for the official photographer.

'It's up to me,' Luke said to himself, gazing in awe at the world-famous trophy. 'I've just got to do something to stop it being pinched.'

Luke's dad had washed the Swifts' all-gold kit in the hostel laundry room and issued a warning as he dished it out to the players. 'Don't get this dirty, lads. You've got to wear it again this afternoon.'

Luke was changing in silence in a corner of the dressing room when he suddenly realized that his teammates were all staring at him.

'Um . . . what do you want?' he said, as if coming out of a trance.

'We're waiting for you to do your little party piece,' said Sanjay.

'Oh, leave it, not important, off you go. I'll join you in a minute.'

The Swifts looked at each other in astonishment. They had never seen Luke so downbeat before a game of football.

'Cheer up, Skipper, it's your birthday,' said Gary.

'What's this party piece?' asked Jon.

'He goes, "Right, men. All ready?" and we go, "Ready, Skipper!" ' Brain explained. 'We always do it before a match.'

'Doesn't matter if we give it a miss for once, does it?' snapped Luke. 'Look, I've just got things on my mind, OK? I'm not in the mood.'

The others trooped outside, leaving only Jon behind with Luke. 'C'mon, out with it. What's up? You can tell me.'

'I've got to tell somebody or I'll burst. Something terrible's going to happen this morning.' Luke glanced around to ensure they were completely alone and then sat his cousin down. 'Promise you won't let on to anybody?'

Jon nodded. 'Course. Anything you say.'

As Luke unburdened himself about what he'd discovered on the back of his autographed paper, Jon's eyes grew wider and wider.

'You positive, Luke?' he exclaimed. 'You're saying Miller's plotting to nick the F.A. Cup and ransom it for a million quid?'

'You see, even you don't believe me. That's why I haven't told our dads – or even the police. Miller would only deny it and then I'd be the one in trouble for wasting police time.'

Jon gave his habitual little shrug. 'At least

you'd ruin his plans. Miller wouldn't dare do anything after you'd reported it.'

'Yeah, suppose so,' Luke sighed. 'But I don't want to risk it, just in case I *am* wrong. I could never live that down. He was a great player once, you know.'

'Seems like he's just a crook now. He must be really desperate for money to try and pull a stunt like this in front of all these people.'

'I think there might be more to it than that.'

'How d'yer mean?'

'Remember I said he broke his leg in the Cup Final? Well, that injury more or less finished his career. He was never the same player afterwards from what I've read.'

'So?'

'So maybe he's got some kind of grudge against the Cup and this is his strange way of getting his own back on it.'

Jon shrugged again. 'Possible, I guess. Anyway, what are we gonna do about it? You've had more time to think about this than me.'

'Knew I could count on you, Johan,' said Luke in relief. 'Best thing to do, I reckon, is let the snatch actually take place first – but Robbie Miller's not the only one who's got a plan. Listen . . .'

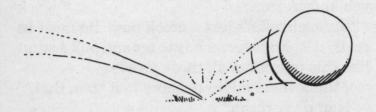

7 At Sixes & Sevens

'Oh, well,' sighed Titch. 'At least we earned a hundred quid.'

The Sparrows – as they were known in the tournament – were on the wrong end of a 5–1 scoreline in the opening game of their three-team group.

'Makes a nice change to get paid for being thrashed,' said Big Ben. 'We usually do it for nothing.'

They had found themselves up against Hartbridge Harriers, the same opponents they were due to meet that afternoon. The Harriers had practised hard for this tournament and it showed. Their slick teamwork was in stark contrast to Luke's makeshift squad, slung together over breakfast, who performed like a bunch of strangers.

Luke himself was virtually a non-playing captain, unable to raise any enthusiasm for the contest. Even his inbuilt commentator was off-duty and the action passed him by in an uncanny silence. Luke's lack of involvement might well have been to their advantage in the Sunday League, but carrying a passenger in a seven-a-side match proved too much of a handicap.

Jon appeared equally distracted, although he did manage to put the ball in the net for a profitable consolation goal. Only the fact that the game was a mere seven minutes each-way saved them from a worse drubbing.

'Waste of time Luke wearing my boots,' grumbled Gregg. 'He could've just wandered about in his slippers.'

They had a while to wait before what was certain to be their second and last game of the tournament. The whole touring party made their way towards the busy photographer, with Luke and Jon trailing along behind.

'What time did you say was on that bit of paper?' asked Jon.

'11.30 – that's during the veterans' challenge match. Clever, eh? Gives Miller a perfect alibi for when the Cup actually gets whipped.'

'By the Pirates?'

'Looks like it,' said Luke, gazing towards a pitch where the students were playing. Someone with a plastic parrot on his shoulder had just blasted the ball over the bar. 'It's not the original F.A. Cup, you know. That vanished from a shop window display. They reckon it was melted down into silver coins.'

Jon was shocked. 'When did that happen?'

'Oh, over a hundred years ago – 1896.'

'Wondered why I hadn't heard about it on the

news,' he sighed. He might have guessed that Luke would know some useless fact like that.

When their turn finally came in front of the camera, the cousins held up the F.A. Cup between them. It was a bittersweet moment. Under normal circumstances, it would have been the soccer highlight of their lives. But it was ruined by the knowledge that, if things went wrong, *they* could be the ones to blame this time for the loss of such a priceless trophy.

Luke astonished his teammates by announcing that he was not playing in the next match. He used the excuse that he wanted to give Titch a full game.

'Must be ill,' muttered Big Ben, tugging on the captain's armband.

'Think I know the real reason,' grinned Tubs, spotting the roaming packs of autograph-hunters. 'If there's one thing that might stop Luke from playing, it's a chance like this to mingle with all them old stars he's always banging on about.'

Tubs wasn't too far wrong, but Luke also needed to be free to keep an eye on Miller and the Pirates. He only watched the first few minutes of their game against the Red Dragons

before slipping away. His absence wasn't noticed until there was nobody to give the half-time team talk, and by then they were 2–0 down.

'Told you,' Tubs said triumphantly. 'Luke's over there, look, trying to get some bloke's autograph. He doesn't care what's happening to us.'

'Who is it?' asked Brain.

'Dunno. He's so old, he must have died before we were born!'

Luke was in his element, surrounded by so many ex-internationals. He recognized most of them, despite their disguises of paunches, glasses and bald heads. He'd already collected five autographs in the back of his notebook when he saw Miller talking to the Pirates.

'The double-crosser!' Luke cursed. 'Bet they've got no idea what he's really up to. They probably think it's just a publicity stunt for charity or something. Huh! The only cause he's interested in helping is his own.'

Meanwhile, Luke's neglected 'Swallows' were staging a comeback. Jon weaved in and out of a couple of tackles and set up his Italian cousin for a pop at goal. Ricki almost put it over the crossbar, rugby-style, but the ball dipped at the last moment, clipped the underside of the woodwork and buried itself in the netting.

'Great goal, Ricki!' cried Big Ben. 'That's a plenty big hole in Miller's wallet. Let's have another now.'

They certainly had their opponents worried. Titch's fierce tackling in midfield had snuffed out the flames of the Dragons' attacks and Gary found space to move forward and support Brain up the left-flank. For a while the Dragons resisted, but finally caved in and surrendered their lead.

The equalizer was well deserved. Gary and Brain linked up neatly along the touchline until the winger had a clear sight of goal. His aim was lethal. Before any defender could close him down, Brain drove the ball low into the gap

between the keeper and his near post. The ball seemed to pick up speed off the wet grass and left the keeper groping.

'Double your money, Miller!' roared Tubs from the touchline. 'The Sparrows are flying high!'

The game ended as a 2–2 draw, confirming the Harriers as group winners and destined for a clash with Tibworth All Stars in the Final.

'D'yer reckon Luke might stand down again this afternoon?' said Titch. 'We might give the Harriers more of a fight of it then.'

'No chance!' laughed Tubs. 'You'll have to put up with both him and me again in the full team.'

Jon left the others to celebrate their mini-success. He pulled on his tracksuit top and went to find Luke at their pre-arranged meeting place in the car park. 'Drew, two each,' he reported. 'Did OK without you.'

'What do you mean by that?' Luke snorted.

Jon tried to rephrase his remark more kindly. 'I mean, your team did well to overcome the loss of their skipper,' he smiled. 'Your fighting spirit must have rubbed off on them. They did you proud.'

'Should think so too after all my coaching. Miller's gonna regret the day he tangled with the Sparrows, er . . . I mean the Swifts.'

'Did you find out anything more?'

'Well, I saw the Pirates moving their minibus into a different position facing the trophy table. I think I know what's likely to happen now. I'll tell you on the way to the summerhouse. We'd better go and get in position before things hot up round here.'

Using the cluster of vehicles in the car park to shield their furtive exit, the cousins disappeared round the side of Tibworth Manor. The rear gardens were more extensive than they had imagined.

'So where's this summerhouse of his?' said Jon as they trotted through the trees.

'How should I know? His diagram wasn't to scale, you know. He'd just drawn some arrows pointing to it on the map, so I'm assuming that's where they're going to stash the Cup. Can't be too far away.'

They found the small stone building nestling in bushes close to a country lane that ran along the length of the estate. Luke was all for going up immediately to check what was inside, but Jon held him back.

'Let's wait here under cover for a bit, OK? Y'know, stake the place out like they do in films – just in case.'

'In case of what?'

'Dunno. Just in case . . .' said Jon. 'Miller must realize the grounds will be searched by the police. He could have his own men lurking about, ready to take the Cup somewhere safer after it's been dumped here.'

'Hmm, good thinking, Johan,' Luke admitted, wishing he'd thought of that himself. They might have walked straight into an ambush.

The exhibition game, England versus Scotland, was now entertaining the spectators before the various Finals took place. The veterans had lost few of their ball skills and the generous applause carried to the boys as they crouched behind some shrubs thirty metres from the summerhouse.

'Sorry to be missing that,' murmured Luke, his breathing rapid and shallow. 'I'd have loved to see all those great players in action . . .'

He paused. Angry cries drifted across the gardens, much different to the previous crowd noises.

'Guess the Pirates have struck,' said Jon. 'If you're right, they should show up here in a couple of minutes.'

'This is it!' hissed Luke, unable to contain his excitement. He was trembling from head to

studded boots. 'Get ready to repel boarders!'

The pirate raid had lasted no more than twenty seconds. As the minibus skidded to a halt beside the table, two of the students jumped out, snatched the trophy and dived back in. By the time either the photographer or security guard could react, the driver was already revving away. He ploughed across one of the pitches, gouging deep tyre tracks in the soft earth as he headed for the front gates.

Few of the spectators enjoying the football were even aware of the drama at first. Nor were the players – except for one. Robbie Miller watched the minibus roar off down the road, and then had to wipe the grin from his face as one of

the tournament organizers raced towards him.

'Sorry, guys, got to go,' he excused himself, calling for a substitute to take his place. 'Something must have cropped up.'

'They've stolen the F.A. Cup!' the official wailed.

'What! Who have?' growled Miller.

'Pirates, Mr Miller – I mean, some of the students . . .'

'Stop babbling, man. What did they look like?'

'Er . . . one had a patch over his eye, and the other was wearing a three-cornered hat with a parrot on his shoulder . . .'

His voice trailed away as he realized how ridiculous that sounded.

'Och! The police are gonna love those descriptions,' Miller said sarcastically, as if genuinely angry. 'Can't wait till I see the thieves' photo-fit pictures on TV!'

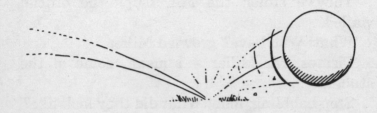

8   April Fool

The minibus pulled up on the country lane next to a padlocked gate. Luke and Jon ducked further down in the shrubbery, but the students were in too much of a hurry to check whether anybody else was about.

A couple of them climbed over the gate with the Cup, ran towards the summerhouse and disappeared inside. Seconds later, they were sprinting for the bus, empty-handed, and it accelerated away in a cloud of exhaust fumes.

'Right, time for us to move quick too,' said Luke. 'Let's go and grab the Cup before any real baddies get here.'

'What if they're already here, watching and waiting like us?'

'All the more reason for acting now,' Luke urged. 'C'mon, we'll just have to chance our luck.'

They left their shelter and broke into a crab-like jog across the open space to the summerhouse. Only upon reaching its stone wall did they remember to breathe again.

'Hear anything?' gasped Jon.

'Only my heart thumping. Or is that yours?'

'Best if one of us stays outside to keep a lookout. You or me?'

'You,' said Luke. 'I'm going in. Keep me covered, OK?'

'What with? Just go and get it, will you, and then we can leg it fast. I'll whistle if I see anybody.'

Luke barged through the door and immediately stumbled over a broken chair. 'I'm OK,' he called out. 'It's just a bit dark in here.'

The building clearly wasn't in use much, apart from as a store for old garden furniture and machinery – and now the F.A. Cup. It stood on the floor in the far corner behind a rusted lawnmower.

Luke would never view the trophy the same way again. It was like finding a beautiful

princess sleeping in the slums. Whenever some victorious team captain proudly held the F.A. Cup up high in front of the royal box at Wembley Stadium, he would picture it among the dirt and debris of this dingy room.

'C'mon, hurry up,' Jon hissed. 'Are you posing with it in there?'

It broke the spell and Luke's fanciful mind clicked back into gear. He lifted the Cup carefully, making sure he didn't scratch it against the mower, and then made for the door.

Jon tried to whistle, but his mouth had suddenly gone dry. 'Wait . . .' he croaked but it was too late. Luke was already stepping outside.

Two men were clambering over the gate from the lane. As they landed on the grass and turned, they saw the boys too. Or at least the back of them. The cousins were in full flight through the tangle of bushes, fleeing in the general direction of the manor. Luke had pushed the heavy, circular base into Jon's midriff and was carrying the rest himself, Cup under one arm and its lid in his other hand.

'Hey! Come back!' came a yell, but they were in no mind to obey.

Then came another command. 'Stop or I'll shoot!'

That one made them think for a moment – but not stop and think. They charged on, heaving for breath in their panic, expecting any moment the sound of gunfire and a whistling bullet. They wouldn't have had time to read whose name might have been on it.

They heard nothing but a lot of swearing. If Tubs had been with them, they might have had a problem, but both Luke and Jon were fitter than their pursuers. And the fear of being caught spurred them on to set Olympic qualifying times for any sprint event that involved carrying silverware.

They didn't stop running until they reached the manor house itself. The boys leant against its red-brick walls to try and recover their breath and their shattered nerves. There was no sign of anyone behind them.

'Reckon . . . they were . . . bluffing . . . 'bout the gun . . . ?' gasped Jon.

'Dunno . . . but . . . think we've . . . lost 'em . . .' gulped Luke, sliding down the wall to sit on the gravel. 'We won . . . Johan . . . we won the Cup!'

It was painful to laugh. Their lungs didn't yet have enough air in them. As their pulse rates gradually subsided, Jon posed another question

that was beginning to bother him. 'So . . . what do we do with it now?'

Luke looked up and blinked. He hadn't thought his own plan through as far as that. 'Put it back on the table?' he said lamely.

'Oh yeah? We casually stroll up and say, "Oh, look what we've just found!" Come off it.'

'Hmm, I see what you mean. Tricky, this.'

'Could be your chance to play the big hero. You'd be on the telly and all the front pages – *The Birthday Boy who saved the F.A. Cup*.'

'Not just me. Both of us,' said Luke, conjuring up even more dramatic headlines. 'It'd be like Pickles all over again.'

'Pickles?'

'Yeah, you know, the dog which went out for a walk one day in 1966 and found the missing World Cup. He became famous.'

'Is that what you want? Fame?'

Luke was sorely tempted, but then gave a heavy sigh and scrambled to his feet. 'No, not really – well, not yet, anyway. Too much explaining to do. I just want to go and play football this afternoon.'

'Good,' said his cousin with relief. 'C'mon, let's just dump the Cup where somebody will soon find it.'

'Another Pickles-wannabe, perhaps. That'd make a good story.'

They crept back into the car park, twice having to dodge down out of sight behind vehicles as somebody approached.

'We can just stick it up on one of the car bonnets and melt away into the crowd,' said Jon.

'OK, but hold on. Wait a minute. I've had an idea.'

Jon groaned. 'You and your ideas. Look, if you ever decide to go on another tour, just leave me out of it, right. I prefer a quiet life.'

Luke had ripped a page out of his notebook and rested it on the ground while he scribbled something. 'Ready now. Let's do it.'

The base and the trophy, complete with lid, suddenly appeared on a bonnet, with a torn piece of paper trapped underneath. The message read:

The F.A. Cup was soon whirling away into the sky to return to the dull safety of the club's trophy cabinet. Its adventures were over.

The tournament was over too. The Finals had been duly completed and Robbie Miller had the small consolation that his All Stars team had defeated the Harriers 3–1. He had not, otherwise, had a good day. Even his beloved Scotland had lost 4–2.

He didn't understand at first how the plan could have failed and how the Cup had turned up again in the car park. Then his men told him of the two boys at the summerhouse. His heart sank. A frantic search of his pockets confirmed his worst fears. The paper with all his notes on was missing.

'That autograph yesterday,' he remembered. 'That idiot Sparrows captain who knew all about me – and who now knows even more!'

Miller found Luke eating a picnic lunch on a grassy bank with his teammates and indicated that he'd like a private word.

'Now then, laddie, have you still got that piece of paper I gave you?'

Luke knew that feigning ignorance would be a waste of time. 'You mean the one with your autograph on it? And something on the back . . . ?'

The subject of their conversation did not need to be mentioned. Miller forced a crooked smile, struggling to control his temper. He knew full well that this boy could make things very nasty for him. 'Aye, that's the one. I trust nobody else has seen it? Like your pal, for instance . . .'

Luke shook his head and Miller eyed him suspiciously, uncertain whether to believe him. 'Aye, good. Well, I'd like it back – please. I'm willing to pay you quite a lot of money for it.'

'I don't want your money, Mr Miller,' Luke replied seriously. 'But I'm sure an extra donation to the students' charities would be appreciated. That might help to keep the Pirates quiet if the police question them.'

Miller nodded. He knew when he was beaten, even though Luke finally confessed that the vital evidence had been destroyed. Just to be on the safe side, Miller produced something from

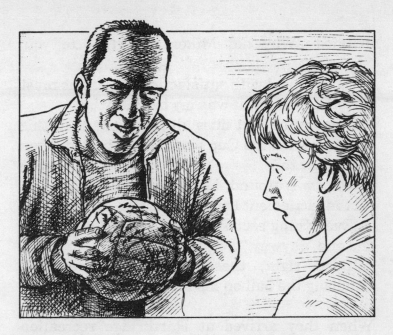

his sports bag that he hoped would ensure Luke's silence too. It was the football used in the exhibition match, signed by all the stars, including Miller himself.

'Our wee secret, eh, laddie?' he said, handing over the souvenir ball.

It was an offer that Luke could not refuse. He sat nursing the football next to Brain on the minibus for the short drive to Hartbridge. The winger was admiring all the autographs, despite the fact that he couldn't read any of them.

'Their writing's worse than mine,' Brain

grinned. 'Why did Miller give this to you, Skipper?'

Luke smiled with satisfaction. 'Guess he must have known that it was my birthday.'

'Hope you didn't miss all the excitement this morning with the Cup and that. Where did you disappear to?'

'Oh, I was around,' he said casually. 'And I had all the excitement I needed, thanks, don't worry.'

'Everything seems to have worked out OK in the end, anyway.'

'Dead right, there, Brain,' he chuckled, bouncing the ball on his lap.

When they arrived at Hartbridge recreation ground, the Harriers captain came up to challenge them. 'What are you lot doing here? We're playing the Swifts this afternoon.'

'That's us – and we're here for revenge!' Luke replied. 'Swifts are much quicker and more skilful than sparrows.'

The Swifts soon discovered that their skipper was back to his usual bubbly self. Luke flitted about the changing room, reminding everybody of their positions in the 4–3–3 formation he had devised to accommodate Jon. Gregg was not best pleased to be among the subs.

'Just a temporary sacrifice for the good of the team, Gregg, OK?' Luke wheedled. 'You'll be on at half-time, promise.'

The player-manager had to work hard to convince their regular striker that it wasn't just because he needed to borrow his boots again.

'Right, men,' cried Luke to gain everyone's attention. 'All ready?'

'Ready, Skipper,' they responded loudly.

'Welcome back, Skip,' laughed Dazza. 'You sound on form again.'

'I just don't know how we managed without you earlier,' said Sanjay, doing well to keep a straight face. 'Got it all sorted, did you, whatever was bothering you?'

Luke glanced at Jon who gave him a little warning shake of the head. They'd agreed not to tell *anybody* about their dramatic rescue act.

'Yeah, no problems. Now today's my birthday and I want . . .'

He was interrupted again, this time by Tubs. 'Is it, Skipper? Oh, you should have said. We'd have got you something.'

Everyone burst out laughing. Luke had only mentioned his birthday about a thousand times since the tour was first arranged.

'Anyway,' he continued, 'I want us to celebrate

with a win and end the tour on a high note . . .'

Sean let out a piercing shriek, making them all cover their ears.

'What the hell was that for?' gasped Sanjay.

'That's about as high a note as I can reach,' he grinned.

'About time your voice broke, then,' Mark muttered, as deeply as he could manage.

Luke gave up. 'OK, men, let's just get out there and show these Harriers how the Swifts can really play.'

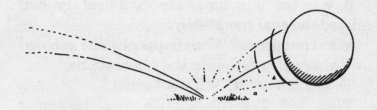

9   Un-Friendly

Luke was determined to enjoy himself in this match now that he could concentrate purely on football again. Although it was a strain to keep the secret bottled up, his commentary at least gave him a broadcasting outlet as a safety valve. After all, nobody was listening.

'The unsung hero of the morning, Luke Craw-ford, kicks off the final game of the Swifts' eventful Easter tour and the ball goes out to Dazza on the right-wing. It has been an amazing birthday for the skipper. If it weren't for him, the F.A. Cup would . . .'

He broke off. He suddenly realized that the ball was in the back of the Harriers' net. Luke had been so concerned with setting the scene and getting in an early mention of the Cup that he hadn't even started to describe the action.

It was too late now. His commentary had missed the goal completely.

'What happened? What happened?' he gabbled as Gary ran by to join in the celebrations.

'Didn't you see it? What a header!'

'Who by? Tell me!' Luke was becoming desperate, but Gary was gone.

Luke followed and threw himself onto the top of the mêlée of gold shirts. Only as the bodies began to part did he discover that cousin Ricki was at the bottom of the pile.

'Brill, Ricki!' cried Luke. 'How did you do it?'

Ricki looked dazed, partly through oxygen starvation underneath the crush. 'Eh? Not me. I no score.'

'Well, who did then?'

'Their number five. Plenty great own goal!'

The Harriers' central defender was still sitting on the grass in disbelief. He had risen to meet the winger's cross and hadn't expected the aerial challenge that put him off. The ball glanced off the side of his head into the far corner of the net,

leaving the goalkeeper speechless – if only for a few seconds. His teammate was making up for it now, standing over him and still finding new, colourful ways of abusing the big defender.

Ricki deserved the credit for his part in the shock goal. Only someone with his level of fitness would have reached the goalmouth in time to leap high for Dazza's overhit centre and force the error.

The blue-shirted Harriers were quick to vent their anger at conceding such a goal. The captain's father had volunteered to referee this

so-called friendly game and he turned an indul-gent blind eye to the many fouls committed, especially by his son.

'*Looks like the Swifts are up against twelve men here,*' muttered the commentary. '*The player-manager will have to make sure that his own team don't retaliate or things could turn ugly. The Swifts must keep trying to play good clean football . . .*'

Luke hopelessly mistimed his next tackle. He stuck out a leg as an opponent dribbled past him, missed the ball, but not the player. The attacker crumpled to the ground as if shot by a sniper – and the ground happened to be inside the penalty area.

'Accidental, ref, honest!' Luke claimed as the man pointed to the spot. 'I went for the ball.'

'No arguing, lad. You're lucky not to get sent off.'

The penalty-taker sent Sanjay the wrong way to level the scores and the rot set in. By half-time the Swifts were in an all-too-familiar position.

'Oh, well, only losing 3–1,' said Mark. 'Could be worse.'

'It usually is,' sighed Big Ben. 'Skipper's only managed to trip one of them up in the area so far.'

Luke pulled a face. 'Can't help it. I don't do it on purpose.'

'Could have fooled me,' grunted Tubs. 'Just how many pens have you given away this season, Skipper?'

'Bet that's one statistic he doesn't keep in his little black book!' Sanjay scoffed. 'Boy, would I love to get a read of that! It must be hilarious.'

Luke had deliberately not brought his official record book on tour. He was frightened of it falling into the wrong hands – Sanjay's, for instance. He knew it was one thing that the goalkeeper wouldn't let slip through his fingers. Not like the third goal.

'They're just a bunch of dirty foulers,' complained Titch. 'Should've had a penalty ourselves when Brain got kicked up in the air.'

'It shows we've earned their respect,' Luke said in encouragement. 'Teams only bother kicking opponents they think can outplay them.'

'Reckon I'd rather not be kicked,' said Dazza. 'Respect is too hard on the shins.'

'Well, you can rub them better this half,' replied Luke. 'Gregg's playing on the wing now, OK? He can't wait to get kicked about.'

There was a lot of fuss as Gregg demanded his boots back. Dazza's were much too big for Luke,

but Sean was coming off too and was reluctantly persuaded to part with his.

'Only if you clean them up during the holidays,' he insisted. 'And make sure you do a good job of it too, Skipper.'

Luke himself had been a target for Harriers' cloggers, mainly because they were fed up of having his commentary buzzing in their ears like an irritating insect that won't go away. Luke borrowed Sean's shinpads too and fastened them inside his socks as a double layer of protection.

The second half began in similar vein. Luke was painfully floored in the centre-circle by a sly kick, but it was difficult to keep him quiet. He bounced back up, as always, and resumed his commentary just as Brain and the ball had been deposited unceremoniously over the touchline together. All they got was a throw-in.

'Disgraceful decision by the referee! Undeterred, Ricki throws the ball in to Brain who bravely takes on the defender again and this time slips the ball through his legs. A perfect nutmeg. That's the way to hit back. Johan's on the ball now just outside the area. He's been having a bit of a quiet game so far, but this looks dangerous – ohhh! Referee!'

Jon had been crudely scythed down by the number five and at last the referee could find no excuse not to give a free-kick. Luke positioned the ball just inside the 'D', a little to the left of centre of the goal, as the Harriers formed a defensive wall.

'That's nowhere near ten yards,' Luke claimed. 'Move them back, ref.'

The appeal was ignored.

'Deaf as well as blind,' muttered Brain, the Swifts' dead-ball specialist, but Jon wanted to take this kick himself.

Luke saw the glint in his cousin's eye and knew he meant business. The foul had riled him.

'The Harriers may live to regret what they've just done,' murmured the commentary, *sotto voce* for a change, so as not to forewarn the opposition. *'They've woken up Jon Crawford, the Swifts' multi-talented guest star.'*

'Doesn't matter about the wall, Luke,' Jon told him. 'The ball's going over it into the top corner.'

It did, too. Jon curled the ball with the inside of his right foot up and over the barricade before it dipped late and thwacked into the netting beyond the keeper's dive. It was a touch of real class.

103

Jon ran the show for the next ten minutes and treated the spectators, including the unemployed Sanjay, to the whole range of his wonderful skills. His equalizer came from a sweetly struck left-foot volley as cousin Ricki's chipped pass reached him just inside the area. The goalkeeper didn't even bother to move for this screamer.

'Stop this guy!' cried the captain. 'Kill him before he murders us.'

They couldn't stop him, not now Jon was in this mood. Even his dad had never seen him so hot. He was much too quick for defenders who tried to chop him down, riding their clumsy tackles with balletic grace and dodging any attempts to trip, push and kick him out of his stride.

The Swifts did not have long to wait for Jon's hat-trick goal. Luke fed him the ball in the centre-circle and then watched Jon take off as if chased by a couple of gunmen again. After fleeing from a bullet, the Harriers defence held no terrors for him.

Luke's commentary might have exaggerated slightly in saying that Jon left six opponents trailing in his wake, but nobody was counting. The poor goalkeeper was resigned to his fate. Jon

took great delight in dribbling round him before scoring, teasing him like a kitten with a ball of wool.

The Harriers were now completely unravelled. Although Jon's appetite for goals was at last satisfied, the home team's morale was in tatters and the inspired Swifts comfortably defended the 4–3 lead he had given them.

Even the allowance of extra added time by the referee failed to produce an equalizer and he eventually had to blow the final whistle. The Swifts had won and Jon was carried from the pitch, shoulder-high, in triumph.

It was a happy, noisy journey home in the crowded minibus. The weekend trip had turned out better than Luke would have dared to predict. He was tucked up by a window, contentedly mulling over what he was going to write for his next report in the *Swillsby Chronicle*, the monthly village newspaper edited by Uncle Ray.

When they stopped at a service station for petrol and refreshments, Luke suddenly found himself the centre of attention. Tubs handed over a brown paper bag.

'Here you are, Skipper,' he grinned. 'Happy birthday from all your teammates. Sorry it's not wrapped or anything.'

Luke opened the bag and pulled out a large, black notebook. He looked up at them in surprise.

'Hope this might make up for your soaking this morning and show we love you really,' laughed Sanjay.

'What's it for?'

'Next season, stupid. So you'll be able to write up all the details of our matches then as well. You must've nearly filled the old one by now.'

'You mean you still want to play for the Swifts next season?'

'Course we do,' said Big Ben. 'Even if we do end up getting relegated. Who else would have us useless lot, eh?'

Luke could not have had a better birthday present. Even the ball and Cruyff's number 14 shirt paled by comparison. Nothing could mean more to him than having the support of his teammates, even if they did sometimes have a strange way of showing it.

'You're not useless,' he said, fighting back the tears he felt welling up inside. 'Far from it. To me, you're all soccer stars!'

THE END

CRAWFORD'S CORNER

Hi! Luke Crawford here again. Hope you enjoyed reading about the Swifts' Easter tour and my adventures with the F.A. Cup. You now know that you'll have me to thank if you ever get the chance to hold up that famous trophy on Cup Final day in front of the royal box at Wembley Stadium. Come on, admit it, I bet you've dreamt of that, haven't you? All soccer mad kids do.

Some great players have actually had that proud moment, but not many of the ones featured here in *Crawford's Corner*. Yep, this is the part of the book where they let me write my own piece without the author or anybody getting in the way. I don't even give Uncle Ray the chance to edit it. He'd only want me to change things, like with my match reports for his newspaper, the *Swillsby Chronicle*. This is straight from me to you.

I want to tell you this time about some of the old

soccer stars, just like the ones whose autographs I got in this story. (Not Robbie Miller, though. Best to leave him out of this after what happened!) I think it's important for all young soccer fans to know something about the really great players who have graced the 'beautiful game', as football is often called. I've had to do some research on this subject in all my soccer reference books as I've decided to stick just to men who have now had to hang up their boots. Modern players like Ronaldo, Roberto Carlos, Giggs, Zidane, Del Piero, Bergkamp, Shearer, Maldini, etc., etc., might well be very good – but true *greatness* has to stand the test of time. We'll have to let history be their judge.

It's been dead fascinating to read all about such stars again. Why not get down to your local library and borrow a book or two yourself to find out lots more about these 'golden oldies'?

Let me start you off. Bet you can't guess who I reckon is the greatest footballer of all time! No, not Pelé. I'll come to him later. You know who I mean really – the fantastic, magnificent, supreme **Johan Cruyff** of course, often known as the Flying Dutchman. My mates say I'm always going on

about him – and why not? I could write a whole book about his wonderful talents. In fact, I probably will do one day when I'm a soccer journalist.

Pelé might well be the most *famous* footballer in the world but – in my opinion at least – the *best* has surely got to be my hero, Johan Cruyff. He's even been a top coach after his fabulous playing days were over, winning four Spanish league championships in a row for Barcelona and also the European Cup. (That's the competition we now call the Champions League.) He played for Barcelona, too, after leading Ajax to three successive European Cup triumphs in '71, '72, & '73. He won the '72 Final virtually on his own, destroying Inter Milan with his skills and scoring both goals in their 2–0 victory. No wonder he was voted European Footballer of the Year three times. Johan also skippered Holland brilliantly in the '74 World Cup in West Germany, scoring the decisive second goal in their 2–0 semifinal win over the holders, Brazil. Unluckily, the Dutch lost 2–1 in the Final itself to the Germans.

Johan Cruyff was the complete footballer. He had everything: pace, acceleration, instant ball control, amazing balance and superb passing

skills – and he also scored loads of goals. He was so versatile and original, even inventing a new ingenious piece of dribbling trickery that had never been seen before. Well, he *was* a genius. It's now known as the 'Cruyff Turn'.

I'd better move on to somebody else, I guess, before I get totally carried away. If there was one player who made a shirt number more celebrated than Johan's number 14, it must be the number 10 of Brazil's Edson Arantes do Nascimento. Who? **Pelé**, of course. A bit easier and quicker to scrawl in autograph books, that's for sure. Many Brazilians are better known by their nicknames, although Pelé doesn't know where his came from. He didn't even like it at first, getting into fights at school when other kids teased him with it. In his own family, he's still called by a different pet name altogether, Dico. There you are, another bit of useful soccer trivia for you to come out with one day and impress all your mates.

Pelé had a phenomenal goalscoring record, notching up 1,283 goals at an average of almost one a game, including 97 in 111 internationals – more than twice as many as anyone else. I'd be proud of

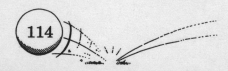

that! Not bad when you consider he struggled with a knee injury most of his long career. He's also the only player to have won three World Cup winners' medals – in '58 (scoring twice in the Final as a seventeen-year-old), '62 and '70. Born into poverty, Pelé's rise to fame and fortune is a real fairy tale. Even a war in Nigeria was stopped for a two-day truce so that both armies could watch him in action.

They are my top two stars of all-time, but the third must be **Alfredo Di Stefano** who played for both Argentina and Spain and who was the idol of the young Johan himself. There can be no greater praise than that as far as I'm concerned. Di Stefano was possibly the greatest all-round forward of his generation and dominated European football in the 1950s and early 60s. He inspired the legendary Real Madrid side to win the European Cup five seasons on the trot from 1956, scoring in every Final and claiming a hat-trick in Real's 7–3 demolition of Eintracht Frankfurt in the last one at Hampden Park, Glasgow, in 1960. His strike partner, the tubby Hungarian with the lethal left foot, **Ferenc Puskas**, grabbed the other four goals in what some people say was the greatest football match ever. What a

pair Di Stefano and Puskas were! Puskas got another hat-trick in the '62 Final and scored an incredible 83 goals in 84 internationals.

Like most great players, Di Stefano worked hard, too, and had tremendous stamina as well as super ball skills. Another player with all those qualities was an Englishman, the late, great **Duncan Edwards** who was tragically killed, aged only 21, in the Munich air disaster in 1958. If Edwards had survived the plane crash, like Bobby Charlton, then he might well have been the England captain to lift the World Cup trophy eight years later.

Did you know there's been a survey on the Internet to allow thousands of football fans to vote for their favourite old stars? Their choices were whittled down to twenty-five names by sportswriters for a Hall of Fame Soccer Museum, but they were so biased that six of the top ten were British – ridiculous! And what made it even crazier was that Johan was only at number four!!! Can you believe that? For the record, the first ten on the list were: Pelé; George Best; Bobby Charlton; Johan Cruyff; Bobby Moore; Gordon Banks; Marco Van Basten; Franz Beckenbauer; John Charles; Kenny

Dalglish; with Duncan Edwards next. It's about time somebody like me redressed the balance. My own top ten that follows is much fairer because I'm only choosing one player per country.

1. Johan Cruyff (Holland)
2. Pelé (Brazil)
3. Alfredo Di Stefano (Argentina & Spain)
4. Franz Beckenbauer (West Germany)
5. Bobby Charlton (England)
6. George Best (Northern Ireland)
7. Ferenc Puskas (Hungary)
8. Eusebio (Portugal)
9. John Charles (Wales)
10. Denis Law (Scotland)

What a team they would have made! In fact, I tried to make a team out of them before realizing I'd only got a couple of defenders. I suppose that's my own bias showing through as a striker myself. But nobody would beat that lot, even so. They'd always score more goals than they let in. I would, however, also need a star goalie to make up the eleven, and my choice for that key position would be the huge

Lev Yashin (The Black Panther) of the Soviet Union, as Russia was called in his days. I'm going to save writing about goalkeepers for another time. As my Swifts' teammate Sanjay says, they deserve a special piece all to themselves.

Let me just give you a potted biography of the other players I picked:

* **Franz Beckenbauer**: stylish, unflappable defender who more or less invented the modern, attacking sweeper role for club and country. Won the European Cup three times in a row in the 70s with Bayern Munich and also skippered West Germany to their '74 World Cup success. Coached them to victory in 1990 too.

* **Bobby Charlton**, now Sir Bobby: most famous English footballer with a record 49 goals for his country, one more than Gary Lineker. Cannonball shot with either foot; scored twice to help Manchester United win the European Cup in '68 and a vital member of the '66 World Cup winning England team. Such a modest superstar!

* **George Best**: not modest at all, but a teammate of Charlton and Law in the great United sides of

the 60s. What a fantastic trio they made! Had a pop star image and was perhaps the most naturally gifted British player of the modern era, so quick and skilful. Sadly, his personal problems off the field forced his early retirement.

* **Denis Law** (The King): great goalscorer (over 300 goals) and crowd-pleaser for his bravery, fiery temperament and cheeky grin. Bought by United in '62 for British record transfer fee of £115,000. Wouldn't have bought his big toe these days, would it?

* **Eusebio** (Ferreira Da Silva): first African player to earn a worldwide reputation, great sportsman and goalscorer for Benfica and Portugal. Top scorer in '66 World Cup with nine goals. Emotional, popular player – burst into tears more easily than Gazza!

* **John Charles**: star for Leeds, Juventus, Cardiff and Wales in 50s and 60s at centre-half or centre-forward. Known as the Gentle Giant in Italy where he's still a legend after scoring 93 goals and winning three championships in five seasons with Juventus. Big, strong, powerful man who never got booked or sent off!

Well, that's just about it, I guess. No space left to tell you anything about all the many great players I've reluctantly had to leave out. Fancy having no room to include such magnificent old stars as the ice-cool captain **Bobby Moore**; the sensational, controversial **Diego Maradona**; the 'Wizard of the Dribble' **Sir Stanley Matthews**; the Scottish cult hero **'Slim Jim' Baxter**; the 'Preston Plumber' **Sir Tom Finney**; the German goal-machine **Gerd Müller**; the battling England captain **Billy Wright**; the elegant, intelligent **Danny Blanchflower**; the skilful Frenchman **Michel Platini**; the three 'R's of Italian folklore **Riva, Rivera & Rossi**; and enough exciting Brazilians to beat the Rest of the World on their own! And that's not to mention all the soccer legends from the first half of the 20th century. I'd be at it for ever – and I've still got my school homework to do that's supposed to be handed in tomorrow.

I'll finish off by setting you a bit of enjoyable homework that you might like to try out with your mates sometime. Why don't you attempt to put together a team of outstanding modern players that could form a World XI to take on anybody in the Universe? Best to make that a squad, on second

thoughts, as you're bound to disagree and you'll probably need a few subs if some multi-limbed aliens start cutting up rough! But remember to make it a truly international squad with stars from all over the planet. Football's the *greatest* game in the whole wide world!

   See ya!

                    Luke

FOOTBALL FANATIC
by Rob Childs

'That's it! I can form my own team!'

Luke Crawford is totally soccer mad. Trouble is, his encyclopedic, anorak-type knowledge of the game is not matched by his ball skills on the pitch. Appearances for the school team are rare, but Luke realizes there *is* a way to guarantee himself a regular game of footie. He can form his own team to play in the Sunday League, and then he can pick himself to play centre-forward every single week! All he needs is ten more players . . .

Discover how Luke puts together the *Swillsby Swifts* in this gripping and action-packed introduction to the bestselling *Soccer Mad* series.

'Rob Childs' love for football is obvious and sincere' *Books for Keeps*

PS: Don't miss my piece at the end about how the game itself began!
Luke

0 440 863600

SOCCER MAD
by Rob Childs

'This is going to be the match of the century!'

Luke Crawford is crazy about football. A walking encyclopedia of football facts and trivia, he throws his enthusiasm into being captain of the Swillsby Swifts, a Sunday team made up mostly of boys like himself – boys who love playing football but get few chances to play in real matches.

Luke is convinced that good teamwork and plenty of practice can turn his side into winners on the pitch, but he faces a real challenge when the Swifts are drawn to play the Padley Panthers – the league stars – in the first round of the Sunday League Cup . . .

ISBN 0 440 86344 9

ALL GOALIES ARE CRAZY
by Rob Childs

. . . but some goalies are more crazy than others!

No-one enjoys keeping goal so much as Sanjay Mistry – the regular, if unpredictable, goalie both for the school team and for the Swillsby Swifts, the Sunday league team led by soccer-mad Luke Crawford. But after Sanjay makes a series of terrible match-losing blunders, Luke decides that it's time someone else had a go at playing in goal – himself!

Determined to prove himself as the number one goalie, Sanjay rises to the challenge with some outstanding and acrobatic saves. But Luke's enthusiasm and crazy antics make him a surprisingly serious rival . . .

ISBN 0 440 86350 3

SOCCER AT SANDFORD
by Rob Childs

'We're going to have a fantastic season!'

Jeff Thompson is delighted to be picked as captain of Sandford Primary School's football team. With an enthusiastic new teacher and a team full of talent – not least that of loner Gary Clarke, with his flashes of goal-scoring brilliance – he is determined to lead Sandford to success. Their goal is the important League Championship – and their main rivals are Tanby, who they must first meet in a vital Cup-tie . . .

From kick-off to the final whistle, through success and disappointment, penalties and corners, to the final nail-biting matches of the season, follow the action and the excitement as the young footballers of Sandford Primary School learn how to develop their skills and mould together as a real team – a team who are determined to win by playing the best football possible!

ISBN 0 440 86318 X

BROOKSIE
by Neil Arksey

Imagine being the son of one of England's top strikers . . . Great, yes!

No! Not if, like Lee Brooks, your dad – 'Brooksie' – has suddenly lost form and become the laughing-stock of the whole country.

Lee hates Brooksie for letting him down. And Lee hates having to move to a grotty new home without his dad. With his own on-pitch confidence at an all-time low, he even begins to hate *football*. But then he meets Dent and his mates and the chance is there for him to play again – with a team of seriously talented players. They've just one problem – no pitch!

A cracking football tale, filled with goal-scoring action and dramatic matchplay moments.

ISBN 0 440 863813

All Transworld titles are available by post from:

Book Service By Post, PO Box 29,
Douglas, Isle of Man, IM99 1BQ

Credit cards accepted.
Please telephone 01624 675137, fax 01624 670923
or Internet http://www.bookpost.co.uk or e-mail:
bookshop@enterprise.net for details

Free postage and packing in the UK.
Overseas customers: allow £1 per book (paperbacks)
and £3 per book (hardbacks).